D1265768

Oh, George!

This edition first published in 2006 by
Sea-to-Sea Publications
1980 Lookout Drive
North Mankato
Minnesota 56003

Text © Sue Graves 2003, 2006
Illustration © Ross Collins 2003

Printed in China

Library of Congress Cataloging-in-Publication Data:

Graves, Sue.
  Oh, George! / by Sue Graves
    p. cm. — (Reading corner)
  Summary: George loves to paint everything from the walls to his sister until his father
thinks of a better "canvas" for his art work.
  ISBN 1-59771-000-8
    [1. Painting—Fiction.] I. Title. II Series.

PZ7.G7754Oh 2005
[E]—dc22

                                                                    2004063627

9 8 7 6 5 4 3 2

Published by arrangement with the Watts Publishing Group Ltd, London

Series Editor: Jackie Hamley
Series Advisors: Linda Gambrell, Dr. Barrie Wade, Dr. Hilary Minns
Design: Peter Scoulding

Oh, George!

by Sue Graves

Illustrated by
Ross Collins

SEA-TO-SEA
Mankato Collingwood London

Sue Graves
"I have four children and two cats so my house is very noisy! I teach children and love writing books. I hope you enjoy this one!"

Ross Collins
"I like drawing and watching cartoons, and eating sausage sandwiches. I live in Glasgow in Scotland. Here's me with Willow in the snow!"

George liked to paint.

He liked to paint
the walls.

"Oh, George!"
said Mom.

He liked to paint
the floors.

11

"Oh, George!"
said Dad.

He liked to paint his
sister, best of all!

15

16

"Oh, George!" said
Mom and Dad.

Dad had an idea.

He got some paint, a brush, and a chair.

And George painted
all day long!

Notes for parents and teachers

READING CORNER has been structured to provide maximum support for new readers. The stories may be used by adults for sharing with young children. Primarily, however, the stories are designed for newly independent readers, whether they are reading these books in bed at night, or in the reading corner at school or in the library.

Starting to read alone can be a daunting prospect. **READING CORNER** helps by providing visual support and repeating words and phrases, while making reading enjoyable. These books will develop confidence in the new reader, and encourage a love of reading that will last a lifetime!

If you are reading this book with a child, here are a few tips:

1. Make reading fun! Choose a time to read when you and the child are relaxed and have time to share the story.

2. Encourage children to reread the story, and to retell the story in their own words, using the illustrations to remind them what has happened.

3. Give praise! Remember that small mistakes need not always be corrected.

READING CORNER covers three grades of early reading ability, with three levels at each grade. Each level has a certain number of words per story, indicated by the number of bars on the spine of the book, to allow you to choose the right book for a young reader:

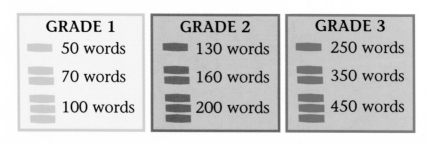

GRADE 1	GRADE 2	GRADE 3
50 words	130 words	250 words
70 words	160 words	350 words
100 words	200 words	450 words